Daisy Dinosaur Gets Lost

by Steve Smallman

Illustrated by
Daniel Howarth

QED Publishing

"See you later!" said Rex.

"Not so fast," said Mum. "I want you to take your sister."

"But Mum!" groaned Rex. "She's too little to come to the swamp!"

"No buts, Rex. Daisy, be good and do what Rex tells you to do," said Mum.

"Come on, Wex!" said Daisy and off they went.

Tubs and Spike were waiting at the swamp.

"Oooooooh, look!" they laughed.
"Rex is holding hands with a girl!"

Rex's face went red.

"Let go of my hand!" he growled.

And Daisy did as she was told.

"She did what you said. Tell her to stand on one leg!" cried Tubs.

Rex was so cross that he told Daisy to stand on one leg.

And Daisy did as she was told.

"This is fun!" said Spike.

"Tell her to pull a face."

"Tell her to hop on the spot."

"Tell her to throw her toy in the air."

And Daisy did as she was told.

"This is boring," said Rex. "Let's climb trees!"

Daisy couldn't even reach the lowest branch.

"Wex," she called. "Hup me, Wex!"

"Hup me, too, Wexy-woo!" laughed Spike.

"Just stay there, Daisy!"
shouted Rex crossly.

And Daisy did as
she was told.

Then the boys played football.

"Can I play Wex?" asked Daisy.

"Yes," said Rex, "and Bogbog can play, too."

"Weally?" said Daisy with a big smile.

"Yes, you can be the goalposts."

Spike aimed for the goal and WHACK!
it hit the post.

"Bogbog!" cried Daisy and ran to pick
him up, just as Rex was about to score.

Rex was cross. So was Daisy.

"Wex, kiss Bogbog better!" she cried.

"GET LOST, DAISY!" he shouted.

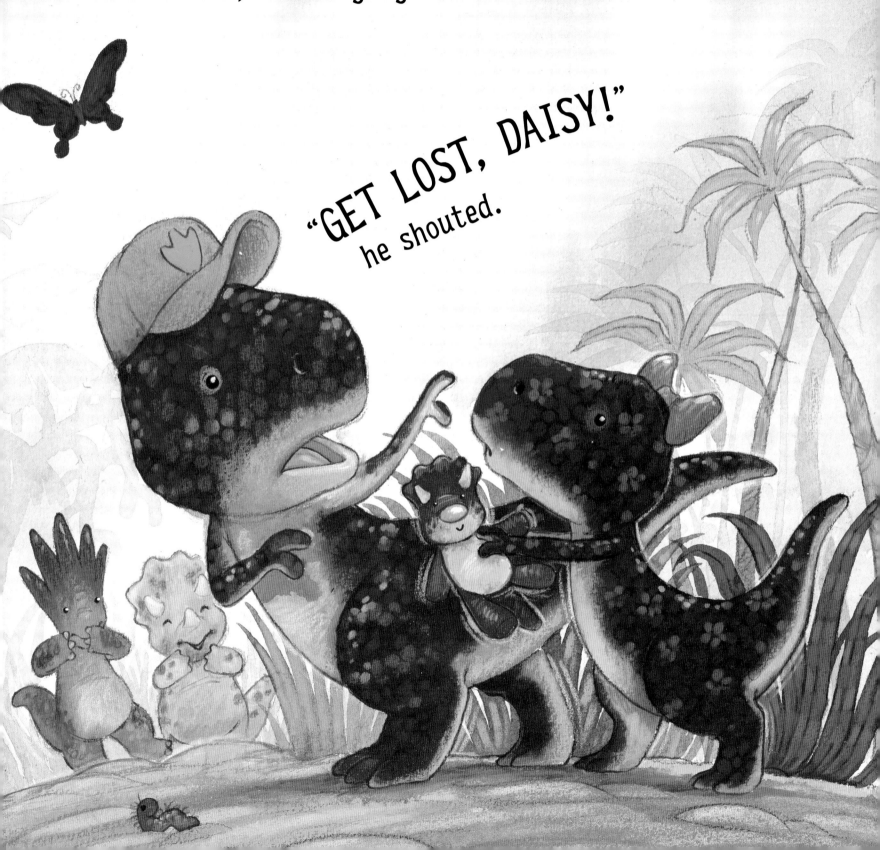

Rex stomped off, red faced, to throw stones into a nearby pond.

Spike and Tubs joined in and soon they were having a great time.

"Come and throw some ploppers, Daisy," called Rex.

But she wasn't there.

"Where's Daisy?" asked Rex.

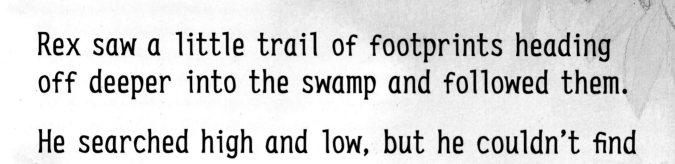

Rex saw a little trail of footprints heading off deeper into the swamp and followed them.

He searched high and low, but he couldn't find her anywhere. Then he heard a noise...

Sniff, sniff...

It was Daisy, sitting underneath some tangled tree roots.

"What are you doing, Daisy?" asked Rex, gently.

"Getting lost," she cried.
"Like you told me to."

"I'm sorry, Daisy," said Rex.
"I didn't mean it."

Daisy cheered up.

"Will you play with me now?" asked Daisy.

"Okay," said Rex, smiling.

"And give me a stompasauwus wide?"

"Ok."

"And throw ploppers?"

"Yes!"

"And kiss Bogbog better?"

"Don't push your luck!"

Notes for parents and teachers

- Look at the front cover of the book together. Can the children guess what the story might be about? Read the title together. Does that give them a clue?

- When the children have read the story or after you have read it to them, ask them which character, Daisy or Rex, was most like them. Did they feel more sympathy for Rex, whose day at the swamp was spoiled, or Daisy, whose big brother wouldn't play with her?

- Why didn't Rex want to take his little sister to the swamp? Would he have minded so much if Spike and Tubs hadn't been there, too? What would the children have done in the same situation? Would it have been any different if he had a little brother instead?

- Rex and his friends played lots of games together. Ask the children what their favourite games are. Discuss which games are fun to play for everyone, no matter if you are big or little, a boy or a girl.

- What does Rex really feel about his sister? How do the children feel about their siblings? If they haven't got any, ask them what they think would be good or bad about having a brother or sister.

- Ask the children to draw a picture of their brother, their sister or themselves as a dinosaur!

Copyright © QED Publishing 2010

First published in the UK in 2010 by QED Publishing
A Quarto Group Company
226 City Road
London EC1V 2TT

www.qed-publishing.co.uk

ISBN 978 1 84835 438 8

Printed in China

Editor: Amanda Askew
Designers: Vida and Luke Kelly